Rapunzel

by Bernice Chardiet
illustrated by Julie Downing

Scholastic Inc.

New York Toronto London Auckland Sydney

ISBN 0-590-42281-2

Text copyright © 1982 by Bernice Chardiet.

Illustrations copyright © 1990 by Julie Downing.

All rights reserved. Published by Scholastic Inc.

Designed by Joan Holub

12 11   0 1 2/0

Printed in the U.S.A.   23

First Scholastic printing, September 1990

To Jane Elizabeth Chardiet
—B.C.

To Jack and Pat
—J.D.

Once upon a time a husband and his wife lived next door to a powerful witch.

The witch had a beautiful garden. There was a high wall all around it. No one ever went there.

But the wife could see over the wall
from her window upstairs.

One day she saw some new green plants
growing in the witch's garden.
They were tender radish plants called rapunzels.
As soon as she saw them,
the wife wanted to eat them.
She wanted them so much,
she would not eat anything else.

She grew thinner and thinner
until her husband said,
"Dear wife, what is wrong with you?"

"Oh, husband," said the wife, "I want some rapunzels.
I want some rapunzels from the witch's garden.
If I do not get some rapunzels to eat, I will die!"

That night, the husband climbed over the garden wall.
He grabbed a handful of rapunzels and took them
home to his wife.

The wife ate all the rapunzels at once.
The next day she begged for more.
So after dark, the husband returned to the witch's garden.
But this time the witch was there.
"Thief!" she shouted.
"Oh, please!" the man said. "I must have rapunzels
for my wife. She says she will die without them."

"Well, then," said the witch.
"Take all the rapunzels you want.
But you must give me something for them."

"I will give you anything you say,"
the man promised.

"Soon your wife will have a child,"
the witch said.
"You must give that child to me!
If you do not, your wife will die."
There was nothing the poor man could do.

A few months later,
the wife had a baby girl.
The witch came at once
and took her away.
And she named the baby Rapunzel.

Each year, Rapunzel grew more and more beautiful.
Her golden hair shone like the sun.
It was so long it trailed on the ground
in a golden path behind her.

On Rapunzel's twelfth birthday, the witch took her
deep into the forest and shut her away in a tower.

There were no stairs in the tower.
There was not even a door.
There was only a window way up at the top.

Every day, the witch
would come to the tower and call:
Rapunzel, Rapunzel!
Let down your hair!

Then Rapunzel would unpin her long, long braid
and let it down from the window.
The witch would grab the end and climb up.

For years, Rapunzel saw no one but the witch.
Then, one day, a prince came riding
through the forest.

He heard someone singing and stopped to listen.
It was Rapunzel singing in the tower.
The prince could not get inside,
but he came back every day to listen
to Rapunzel singing.

One morning, he saw the witch coming.
He hid behind a tree
and heard the witch call:
   Rapunzel, Rapunzel!
   Let down your hair!

Then a long, golden braid came down
from the window, and the witch climbed up.

The prince waited until the witch left.
Then he ran to the tower and called:
   Rapunzel, Rapunzel!
   Let down your hair!

In a moment, the golden braid
came down from the window.
Quickly the prince climbed up.

Rapunzel was frightened of the prince.
But his gentleness won her love.
Soon she agreed to leave the tower and
be his wife. But how could she get out?

"Bring me some strong silk thread,"
she said, "and I will weave a ladder."
So every night when the prince came,
Rapunzel worked on the ladder.
And every day when the witch came,
Rapunzel hid the ladder away.

One day, Rapunzel was very tired.
Without thinking she asked the witch,
"Why don't you climb up like the prince?
He's gentle and quick. You are so slow and clumsy!"
"Wicked child!" screamed the witch.
"What are you saying?
I hid you away here so no one could find you.
What have you done?
You tricked me! You tricked me!"

The witch was so angry, she cut off Rapunzel's
braid! Then she took Rapunzel far away
to a lonely place in the middle of
nowhere — and left her to live or die.

That very same evening,
the prince came and called:
  Rapunzel, Rapunzel!
  Let down your hair!

The braid came down as always,
and the prince climbed up quickly.
But instead of Rapunzel,
there was the witch!

"Your little songbird is gone,"
the witch said.
"You will never see Rapunzel again."

When he heard those terrible words, the prince
jumped from the tower.
He landed in a thornbush, and the thorns
scratched his eyes.
From that moment, the prince was blind.

For years, the prince wandered in the forest.
Then one day, he came to a lonely place
in the middle of nowhere.

Someone was singing. The prince stopped to listen.
The singing grew louder and clearer.
Could it be…?

It was Rapunzel!

Rapunzel knew the prince at once
and ran to meet him.
When she saw he was blind, she began to cry.
Her tears fell on the prince's eyes.
Suddenly he could see again!

The prince took Rapunzel to his kingdom.
There they were married and lived happily
together for a long, long time.